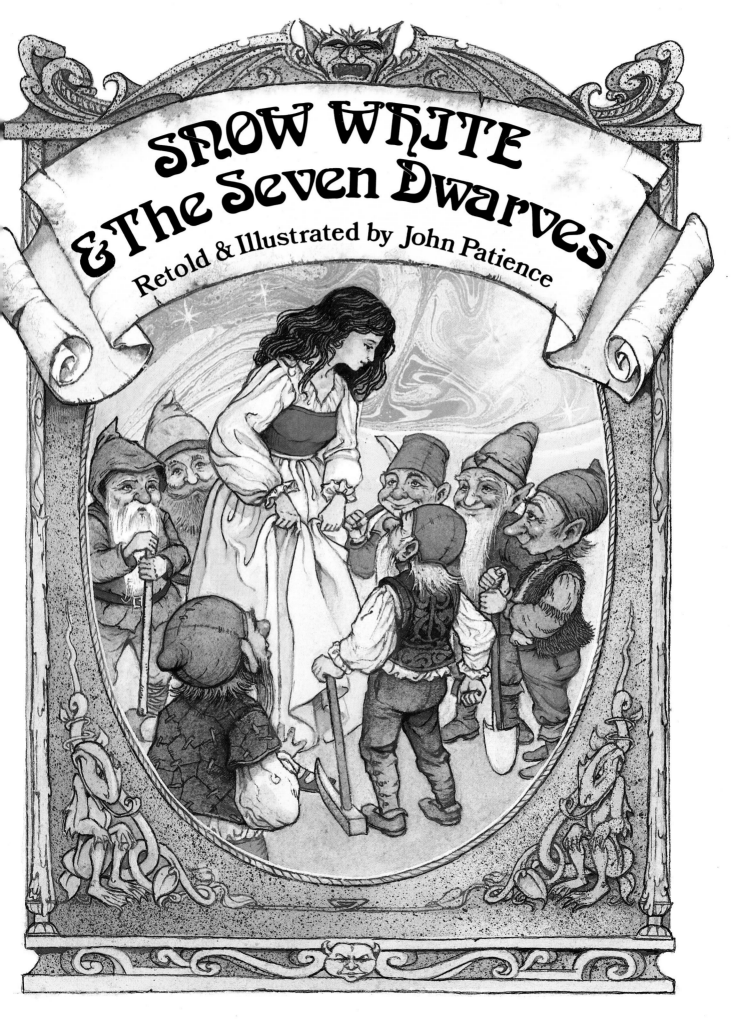

SNOW WHITE
&The Seven Dwarves

Retold & Illustrated by John Patience

Once upon a time a queen sat sewing by her window. Snow flakes were falling outside, and as she watched them settling on her black ebony windowsill, she pricked her finger with the needle and a drop of red blood fell onto the snow. Then she thought to herself, "I wish I had a daughter with skin as white as that snow, with cheeks as red as blood and hair as ebony black as the window frame."

Strangely, the queen's wish came true and she gave birth to a beautiful baby girl whom she named Snow White. But alas the queen died when Snow White was born and before long the king married again.

The new queen was very beautiful but she was evil and vain and could not bear to think that anyone might be lovelier than she. She had a magic mirror which she would look into every day, saying:

"Mirror, mirror on the wall,
Who is the fairest of them all?"
The mirror's answer was always the same:
"Thou art the fairest,"
until one fateful day, when Snow White had grown up, it replied:
"Thou art fair and beautiful to see,
But Snow White is fairer far than thee."
At these words the queen flew into a terrible rage. She called a servant and ordered him to take Snow White into the forest and kill her!

The servant knew he was meant to kill Snow White, but he couldn't do it, so he left her in the forest at the mercy of the weather and the wild beasts.

Soon Snow White began to feel frightened and hungry. She wandered around, looking for berries that she might eat. Suddenly she saw a tiny cottage. She went up to the door and knocked. There was no answer so she went inside. The room was cozy and warm and the table was laid for supper. A stew bubbled in the pot which hung over the fire. The smell was irresistible and Snow White helped herself to some. Then, feeling sleepy, she went upstairs and lay down on one of the seven little beds she found there.

Presently in came the owners of the cottage – seven little dwarfs who worked in the mountains digging for gold. They saw immediately that all was not right; there was a dirty plate on the table! They all crept up the stairs and then one of them whispered, "Look, someone is sleeping in my bed!" His brothers were filled with wonder and astonishment and came with their lamps to look at

Snow White. "Good heavens! What a lovely child she is," they whispered. The dwarfs were delighted to find her and took great care not to wake her, but fussed around as quietly as little mice, tucking her in and making her snug.

The next morning, Snow White told the dwarfs her story and they took pity on her. They decided to let her live in their cottage with them, and in return she could keep the place clean and cook their meals while they were out digging for gold. Snow White soon settled into her new home and was very happy because the dwarfs were much kinder to her than her stepmother had been.

It seemed that Snow White would live happily ever after with the seven dwarfs, until one day her stepmother looked into the magic mirror and asked it who was the fairest in the land.

"Queen, thou art of beauty rare," replied the mirror,

"But Snow White living in the glen,
With the seven little men,
Is a thousand times more fair."

When the queen realized that her servant had deceived her and Snow White was still alive, she was terribly angry. She locked herself in a secret room in the castle and brewed a horrible poison which she put into a beautiful, rosy, red apple. Then, disguised as a gypsy, the queen set out for the dwarfs' cottage.

The evil queen knocked on the cottage door and begged to be let in, but the dwarfs had warned Snow White not to open the door to strangers and so she refused. "Silly girl," said the queen, "I've brought you a lovely apple. Take it."

"Oh, what harm can it do?" thought Snow White. She opened the door and took a bite from the apple. Immediately she fell down dead upon the floor.

When the dwarfs found Snow White they were all heartbroken. They tried every way they could to revive her, but it was no good. At last they gave up hope and made her a beautiful crystal coffin, which they placed in a forest glade. Every day they brought fresh flowers and placed them around the coffin and wept for her.

One day a Prince came riding by. When he saw Snow White he fell in love with her and, opening her coffin, he lifted her in his arms. As he did so the piece of apple which the dwarfs didn't realize was lodged in her throat, fell from her mouth. She opened her eyes and fell in love with the prince at first sight.

The wicked queen could not believe it when her mirror said,

"Oh queen, although you are of beauty rare,
The Prince's bride is a thousand times more fair."
She was so furious that she choked and died.

Now Snow White had nothing to fear from the wicked queen and she lived happily ever after with her prince in a fine palace, where they were often visited by seven dwarfs.